This book belongs to

Bria Dionne Alexander

Published by Advance Publishers
© 1998 Disney Enterprises, Inc.
All rights reserved. Printed in the United States.
No part of this book may be reproduced or copied in any form
without the written permission of the copyright owner.

Written by Lisa Ann Marsoli
Illustrated by Adam Devaney and Diana Wakeman
Produced by Bumpy Slide Books

ISBN: 1-57973-001-9

10 9 8 7 6 5 4 3 2

WHAT A SURPRISE!

The Seven Dwarfs had an unexpected guest. She was the beautiful, kindhearted princess Snow White — and she had chosen their very own cozy cottage for her home. To show them how much she appreciated staying with them, Snow White had cleaned their cottage from top to bottom and cooked them a delicious soup for their dinner.

That night, as they danced and sang along with their new friend, the dwarfs thought how much merrier Snow White made everything seem.

The next morning, Doc asked the other dwarfs to gather round. "Men," he said, "let's do something nice for the Princess today. After all, she's been awfully ice to snus . . . I mean snice to nus . . . that is, nice to us!"

The dwarfs nodded their heads in agreement, and it was quickly decided that they would do all the chores that day. But their lively discussion of who should do what was suddenly interrupted when Snow White appeared at the top of the stairs.

"Well, I see you're all up bright and early," Snow White called cheerfully. She stretched and rubbed her eyes.

"Did you sleep well, Princess?" Happy asked.

"Oh, yes!" Snow White replied. "I was dreaming that my handsome prince carried me off to his castle on a beautiful white horse!"

"Well, you just go right back to sleep and dream!" Doc told her. "We'll see to everything."

Snow White thanked the dwarfs with a sleepy smile and returned to bed.

Downstairs, the dwarfs finished dividing up the chores and set to work. Dopey and Sleepy took charge of fixing breakfast. Sleepy gathered the silverware. In no time at all, his eyes had drooped shut and his snores were filling the cottage.

But Dopey didn't notice. He was too busy concentrating. After all, he had never made gooseberry muffins before.

Dopey got out a large bowl. In it he placed lots of flour, some eggs, a little sugar, and a cup of milk. Then he stirred it all together until it looked wet and lumpy. Next he spooned the batter into a muffin tin and placed the tin in the oven.

Pleased with himself, he picked up a basket and went outside to pick the gooseberries. Poor Dopey! He didn't know he was supposed to gather the berries first. To make matters worse, he didn't know he had to start the oven.

Out by the woodpile, Grumpy was chopping
kindling for the fire. The CHOP CHOP CHOP of
his axe made a rhythm, almost like a little song.

"Hmmm," Grumpy said to himself. "Maybe I'll
make up a tune for Snow White. She did make

supper for us, after all." So he stopped chopping and began to whistle out loud, but after a few notes, he grumbled and started again. But then, Grumpy grumbled over almost everything. That was just his way.

Over by the stream, Doc and Bashful were washing clothes. Doc dunked the laundry in a big tub of soapy water. "Clean as a thistle! I mean clean as a whistle!" Doc said proudly.

Meanwhile, Bashful had rigged up a clothesline by tying a piece of rope between two trees. As Doc handed him the clean clothes, Bashful hung them up.

One by one, Bashful hung up socks, shirts,
and a hat to dry. As each piece of wet clothing was
added, the line sagged lower and lower. Doc handed
Bashful one last pair of pants and strolled past him
toward the cottage.

"Hurry up and finish now!" Doc called.

"We've still got more work to do."

Bashful nodded. Then he carefully placed the pants on the clothesline and turned to follow. The second his back was turned, the line gave way. The clean clothes landed with a SPLOSH on the muddy ground.

In the meantime, Happy and Sneezy were busy
collecting wildflowers in the woods.
"Do you think Snow White will like these?"
Happy asked, holding out a colorful bouquet.

"She sure w–w–w–ACHOO!" Sneezy sneezed. Happy looked down at the flowers. Sneezy's sneeze had knocked all the petals off!

"Gesundheit!" said Happy. "Goodness, Sneezy, this is taking a lot longer than I thought! But no matter. It is a lovely day to be outdoors!" he added brightly.

When Happy and Sneezy finally had enough
wildflowers to take home to Snow White, they
headed back to the cottage. There the rest of the
dwarfs were waiting, restless with excitement.
"Shall I go upstairs and wake the Princess?"

Doc asked. But before the men could answer, a low
buzzing sound filled the cozy room.

"What's that?" wondered Sleepy, who had been
awakened by the noise.

"Sounds like . . . like . . ." Grumpy began.

"Bees!" the other dwarfs shouted together.
They stared as a cloud of the insects rose out of
Happy and Sneezy's bouquet of flowers and began
to fly around in great, buzzy circles.

"What should we do?" wondered Sneezy as one of the insects circled his nose, making it twitch.
"Run!" cried Bashful.

Snow White was awakened from her dreams by the clatter as the dwarfs fled out the door. Then, as she looked around the cottage, she guessed what the dwarfs had been up to. She could see the table and the dirty bowl from Dopey's baking.

"How sweet," she said with a smile. "I don't want to ruin their surprise for me, so I'll just give them a little help." And she set to work.

The first thing she did was make a new batch of muffins, adding the gooseberries before pouring the batter into the tin. Then she put some kindling in the oven and lit it. Soon a cheerful fire glowed inside. "That's better!" she exclaimed as she popped the muffins into the oven.

Next, Snow White picked up the forks and spoons and knives that Sleepy had taken out earlier and put them in their proper places.

Snow White stepped outside the cottage and looked around. Where had all the dwarfs gone? Soon she saw the pile of muddy laundry. Quickly Snow White put the line back up, washed the clothes again, and hung them up to dry.

As soon as she'd finished, she heard the
CRUNCH CRUNCH CRUNCH of leaves in the
forest as the dwarfs marched back to the house.
"Oh, dear!" she said to herself. "I'd better get
back inside — and quickly, too!"

"That's the trouble with flowers," Grumpy
muttered as the dwarfs approached the clearing.
"They look sweet, but inside they're nothin' but trouble!"
"Now, Grumpy!" Doc scolded him, "it's the tees
who caused the bubble — I mean the bees who

caused the trouble — not the flowers."

"Shhh!" Happy warned them as they reached the door to the cottage. "We don't want to wake the Princess up until we're ready!"

"Right!" agreed Bashful as they went in.

Inside, the delicious smell of fresh-baked muffins surrounded them. "Mmmm!" they all agreed, and Dopey silently puffed out his chest with pride.

Sleepy was proud, too. He sat down to admire the table — and promptly fell asleep.

But Doc was too excited to notice. "You men wait down here!" he commanded as he crept up the stairs. "Oh, Princess!" he called, rapping on the bedroom door.

Snow White opened the door, yawning and stretching.

"Surprise!" cried the dwarfs.

"Breakfast is served!" added Doc. He led Snow White downstairs.

"Oh, my!" Snow White said as Bashful pulled out her chair.

"Now, don't you do a thing!" Happy told her. "Today is your day!"

They all sat down to a feast of warm gooseberry muffins. "What a wonderful job you did!" Snow White said appreciatively. The dwarfs smiled. Snow White certainly seemed to be pleased!

After they were done, Grumpy herded them
all over to the organ.

"He made up a song especially for you, Princess,"
Doc told her.

Snow White clapped her hands in delight.

The dwarfs watched as she danced in time to the music.

"Grumpy, isn't that the same song you played last night?" Happy called.

"I thought it sounded familiar," Grumpy muttered.

"Oh, I don't mind!" Snow White reassured him. "I love it just as much this morning as I did yesterday!"

Then Doc told Snow White how they had also chopped the wood and done the laundry so she wouldn't have to lift a finger all day long.

"Thank you," Snow White replied. "Thank you for everything! I may be a princess, but today I feel like a queen!"

It was true she herself had had to bake the muffins and set the table and wash the laundry. But Snow White didn't mind. She had discovered how much her new friends cared for her. "And that," she sighed as she closed her eyes that night, "is the best surprise anyone could wish for."

The Seven Dwarfs decided to
Surprise their friend Snow White,
But things got in a muddle
And she had to set things right.
The Princess didn't mind because
She saw how hard they tried
To show her in so many ways
The love they felt inside.